RED DOG
AN EVIL DEAD MC NOVELLA

NICOLE JAMES

RED DOG
AN EVIL DEAD MC NOVELLA

NICOLE JAMES

Published by Nicole James
Copyright 2016 Nicole James
All Right Reserved
Cover Art by Viola Estrella

CHAPTER ONE

Just across the Northern California border into Oregon —

Four motorcycles sat parked in the gravel, their chrome gleaming in the moonlight. They belonged to members of the Evil Dead MC's San Jose Chapter.

"You sure this is the spot?" Green asked, eyeing the wooded area around them. "We're in the middle of fuckin' nowhere."

Cole lit up his second cigarette since they'd shut off their bikes. He blew the smoke in the air and responded. "Yup. First gravel road off Hwy 99."

Red Dog stood with his hands in his pockets, his gaze on the night sky. "Sure are a fuck-of-a-lot of stars out here."

Only the chirping of crickets, and the sound of an occasional big rig traveling down Interstate 5 in the distance broke the silence.

"It's fucking quiet out here, isn't it?" Wolf noted, taking in a deep breath of fresh night air scented with the smell of pine.

"Too quiet. Where the fuck are they?" Green snapped.

"They'll be here. Chill out, man." Cole took another drag off his smoke, the glowing tip flaring in the dark.

"Thought you said midnight. It's half past. They're late."

"What the fuck are you so jumpy for, Green?" Dog asked. Noting the man's fidgeting, he teased, "You scared of the dark?"

"Fuck off. Just don't like this whole setup. Feels like we're sitting ducks. What the hell was wrong with the old meeting place?"

"Gotta change it up, Green. You know that," Cole replied.

"Yeah, well, who the fuck picked this place?" Green slapped at a mosquito.

Wolf teased him, "You just don't like bugs."

"Fuck no, do you?" he growled, swatting at another. "This place is full of 'em."

The distant unmistakable sound of short drag pipes on a Harley echoed through the night.

Cole, who was slouched sideways on his bike, one boot on the ground, one on the foot peg, stood. He took a final drag and dropped his cigarette, grinding it under his boot. "Show time, boys."

All eyes turned down the gravel road they'd ridden up. The sound grew closer and louder until three headlights rounded the bend, illuminating the dust still hanging in the air in an eerie way.

The bikes stopped, the engines shut off and the headlights extinguished as the new arrivals dismounted. The Oregon Chapter had arrived. The men embraced.

"Sorry, we're late," the one slapping Cole on the back said as he pulled back from the San Jose VP. "Had a tail we had to lose."

"Feds?"

"ATF."

Cole frowned at his Oregon counterpart. "You sure you lost 'em, Weez?"

The man nodded. "Yeah. Doubled back twice. Lost 'em in Medford."

Cole nodded. "Good." He lifted his chin. "You get everything we need?"

"Inside the saddlebags. Sixty and hundred-round magazines."

"How many?"

"Many as we could carry." Weez grinned. "You got your quota of ammo for the month covered. Don't worry."

"Thank God for Oregon." Cole grinned back.

"Yeah, the California ban on high capacity magazines must suck for you guys."

"Well, thanks to our Oregon brothers, we get around it, don't we?"

The men chuckled. Cole nodded for his boys to begin the transfer. Five minutes later, the men were slapping each other on the back in farewell. The San Jose Chapter watched as the three bikes rolled out, leaving a cloud of dust in their wake.

They were about to load up, when Red Dog's phone went off. He pulled it from his pocket and frowned down at the display.

"Who is it?" Cole asked, noting Dog's expression.

"Shane," he replied, answering the call and putting it on speaker. "Yeah," he barked in greeting.

"Your ol' lady is up at Club XS."

Dog frowned, sure he'd heard incorrectly. "What

did you just say?"

"You heard me. She's dressed for pickin' up men and one more drink, she'll be dancin' on a fuckin' table. What do you want me to do?"

Jealousy surged through Red Dog's body like a jolt of electricity, and his jaw clenched as he grit his teeth. "She with someone?"

"I think she's out with some chicks. Ones I've never seen before. If you're asking if there's a guy, don't see one. But that won't last long. She's definitely attracting attention."

Dog growled into the phone, "Get her the hell out of there and take her back home."

"You do realize that requires me puttin' her on the back of my bike, right?"

"Yeah, I know that. You fuckin' touch her, you're dead."

"Brother, I may have to carry her out of here, that's gonna require some touchin'." Dog could hear the grin in Shane's voice. The motherfucker was enjoying this. So were his brothers, judging by the snickering they emitted along with shoulders shaking.

"Just fuckin' get her home." Dog disconnected the call, shoving his phone in his pocket.

"Trouble in paradise?" Cole asked with a grin.

Green guffawed at that. "Paradise? Only paradise Dog's ever gonna see is the Paradise Motel, and there ain't gonna be no seventy-two virgins waitin' for him either."

The guys chuckled.

"Shut the fuck up, Green," Red Dog snapped. "Like you'd know a virgin if she sat on your face."

"I had me one, once," Green insisted, feeling the

need to set the record straight. "Wasn't all its cracked up to be."

"I'm sure she felt the same way about you, Green," Wolf teased.

Cole looked over at Red Dog in all seriousness. "You do something to piss off your ol' lady?"

"Fuck if I know. I'm sure she'll goddamn tell me when I get home."

Wolf chuckled. "Maybe we should stop off and get you a mouth-guard. Wouldn't want her to mess up all that dental work again."

Dog made to lunge at Wolf, but Cole pushed him back with a fist to his chest, laughing. "Let it go, Dog. He won't stop 'till you do."

"He'll stop quick enough with my fist in his mouth."

"Gotta catch me first, bro." Wolf made a kissy face at Dog as he fired his bike up and tore off down the road.

"Let's roll," Cole ordered and they mounted up and followed the trail of dust Wolf left in his wake.

CHAPTER TWO

Shane stood outside the bar, the neon reflecting on his blond hair. He squinted into the distance, taking in the lights of the strip, his phone to his ear. His boots crunched on the gravel as he paced next to his bike, Red Dog's last words coming through loud and clear from 300 miles away.

Jamming his phone back in his hip pocket, he headed back inside the nightclub and made his way through the crowd, cutting a path to where Mary sat at the bar. She hadn't spotted him earlier, so he could only imagine what her reaction would be when her eyes landed on his Evil Dead cut.

He pushed between her barstool and the guy next to her. Her attention was turned to the girlfriend sitting on her other side—one Shane was pretty sure she'd probably come with—so she didn't see him approach.

Mary was a petite Asian beauty with porcelain skin and dark glossy hair that hung to her waist. It was currently pulled to the side, revealing her low-back dress.

"You lookin' for a date, sugar?" he growled low in her ear. That pretty back went ramrod straight as she perhaps recognized his voice. Twisting with the cocktail in her hand, her red nails flashing against the sparkle of the delicate martini glass, her almond shaped eyes hit his leather vest first and then got huge as they made their way up to his face. Her lips parted with a holy-crap expression.

"Hey, Mary." He grinned back at her, a cat-that-caught-the-canary look on his own face.

"Shane," she whispered. "What are you doing here?" Her eyes moved past him, searching the crowd for more Evil Dead members. Finding none, her eyes returned to him, and her body relaxed.

"Seems I could ask you the same question."

"I'm having a drink. Is that against the law?"

"Not exactly. But how do you think Dog's gonna react when he comes home and finds you gone?"

"I really don't care."

"You don't care?" He smiled and shook his head, knowing she was well aware of how the MC worked. Ol' ladies did not just take off to go drinking fifty miles from home, especially not without their ol' man's knowledge. "You ever done this before?"

"Nope."

"What made you do it this time?"

"Something had to snap. I guess it was me."

"Seriously, Mary, tell me."

"I guess I just had enough, Shane. You know everyone reaches that last straw — the one that breaks the camel's back." She shrugged.

"And what was that straw?"

"Look, I know you're club brothers and all, but it's really none of your business."

"Nope, you're right. It's not. What *is* my business is

having my brother's back." That got her attention and changed her nonchalant attitude in a heartbeat.

"Please don't call Red Dog," she pleaded, a thread of panic in her voice.

"Sorry, babe, call's already been made."

Her eyes flashed to the door as if she half expected the club to bust through at any second. "Is he on his way?"

"He's at the Oregon border on club business. Take him probably six hours to get back."

Her delicate chin came up, her long sleek hair falling over one shoulder. "Good. Go about your business then. You ratted me out; your brotherly duty is fulfilled."

"Don't work that way, babe. I got a responsibility to look out for my brother's ol' lady. Dog wants you home, that's where I'm takin' you, sweetheart."

He watched one delicately sculpted brow arch. "I'm not going home, Shane."

A grin pulled at the corner of his mouth. She was cute if she thought she could stop him. He took the drink out of her hand and set it on the bar. "Mary, don't make this difficult. You know I'm takin' you outta here, even if its gotta be over my shoulder. And I'd rather not haul you through this crowd with your ass in the air, but you know I'll do it."

Their eyes locked, and he could see the realization form on her face as she grasped the truth of his words.

"I think you heard the lady. She doesn't want to leave with you."

Shane's head turned, his eyes narrowing on the man behind him. He had an over-the-top spray-tan that looked a sickly orange in the bar light. "Stay outta this, buddy. Only warning you're gonna get."

Mary slid off her stool, grabbing Shane's arm as her eyes connected with the man. "It's fine. I'll go with him."

Shane made to pull free of her grasp, but she squeezed her hand, drawing his attention from the man.

"Don't start trouble. Please." Shane's eyes met her pleading look. He nodded.

"All right. Then let's go."

Unfortunately, Spray-tan Dan had shit for brains. He grabbed Mary's arm. A mistake he'd live to regret.

"The lady is staying here."

Shane decked him with one powerful punch to the jaw that sent the man sprawling to the floor, and then he moved to stand over his prone body. "You don't ever touch an Evil Dead ol' lady. Got that, motherfucker?"

Not waiting for an answer, Shane clamped his hand around Mary's upper arm and pulled her through the crowd and out the bar. His bike was parked up front, so they didn't have far to go. He released her, spinning toward her. "What the fuck, Mary? What the hell are you doing here?"

"What do you care?"

"Dog cares. Therefore, I care."

"To hell with Dog. And to hell with you, too."

"Christ, Mary, cut me some slack. I don't like being in this situation anymore than you do. But here we are." They stared each other down. Seeing he was going to get nowhere with her, he swung his leg over the bike and fired it up. Handing her his helmet, he ordered, "Climb on. Now."

She was fuming, but she took the helmet from him and complied, her short dress hiking up her thighs. When he felt her arms wrap around him, he gunned the throttle and roared out of the parking lot, cursing himself for picking the wrong bar to stop for a drink.

CHAPTER THREE

It was 7:00 a.m. when the boys finally made it back to San Jose and rolled up at Red Dog's house. As they cut their engines and the rumble faded, Cole lifted his chin toward the front door, calling all their attention to it. "Dog."

Red Dog swiveled his head, his eyes hitting the entrance. It stood wide open. "What the fuck?"

All four of them immediately dismounted, pulling their handguns.

"After you, bro," Cole whispered to Dog as they approached the entrance.

They followed him inside, pausing just clear of the door to scan the room, guns lifted.

"Mary!" Dog called out, but received no response. "Billy!"

All that greeted the four men was dead silence.

Red Dog made his way down the hallway to the master bedroom with Cole on his heels. The rest spread out through the house, searching for an intruder. Dog and Cole took in the trashed bedroom. Dresser drawers stood open, empty of all contents. A glance into the closet revealed that most of its contents had been emptied as well.

"What the fuck, Dog, you been robbed?"

Dog moved into the doorway of the walk-in closet. "Suitcases are gone."

Cole watched as he yanked his phone out. A moment later, Dog bit out, "Where the hell is she?"

"I took her home. Dropped her off at 2:00 a.m., bro," Shane replied over the speaker.

"She ain't here."

"Well, that's where I left her. Swear to God, Dog."

Wolf strolled in, taking in the room. "Looks like she packed her shit up and left you, man."

"What the hell did you do this time?" Green smirked, following Wolf into the room. He was holding up a piece of broken dinner plate. "She took a hammer to your wedding china. It's smashed all over the kitchen table like she was making you a fucking divorce mosaic."

"Just shut the hell up," Red Dog snapped. He tried calling Mary, but it went straight to voice mail. Then he tried his son's phone, but got the same. His mind searched for a reason she'd leave him. He could think of nothing he'd done that would warrant this kind of reaction from her. Hell, he couldn't even think of what he'd done that would piss her off at all. Not recently anyway.

Red Dog collapsed down onto the foot of the bed. Running a hand over his face, he tried to make sense of it all. She'd never done anything like this before. From the moment he'd met her, she'd never shied away from telling him how she felt, telling him her mind or telling him off, for that matter. It was one of the things he loved about her. It had surprised him when he'd first met her, that spunk of hers. Hell, most women he'd met in his life were afraid of him, either of the cut he wore or just his six-foot-four size. With his red hair and beard, he reminded most people of a Viking. So, he wouldn't have been surprised when he met the petite china doll, as he called her, if she would have been even more intimidated than most. But was she? Not his Mary. Nope, there wasn't a shy or timid bone in her body.

His mind drifted back to the first time he'd ever laid eyes on her. It had been like a freight train running him over. That's how much she affected him right from the very first instant.

Fourteen years ago...

Red Dog walked into Sonny's Gentleman's Club. It was a strip club that the Evil Dead had an investment in. He was there to pick up their cut of this week's profits; a job that usually fell to Wolf. Red Dog hadn't actually been up here in a long time. He glanced around. A few updates had been made since he'd last been there, new carpet, new lighting and an updated stage. The place was doing well.

Red Dog moved to the end of the bar and caught the eye of the bartender, who lifted his chin at Dog and moved off to let Sonny know he was here. Dog leaned against the bar and waited, his eyes sliding to the stage where a voluptuous blonde was working the pole.

A minute later, the bartender returned. "Sonny knows you're here. He's dealing with a problem in back." The man nodded towards the stage. "He said to make yourself comfortable for about twenty minutes, and he'll be with you as soon as he can. Drinks are on the house."

Dog nodded and ordered a whiskey, then headed over to the end of the stage and took a seat at the rail. The blonde saw him and abandoned the patron she'd been getting dollars from and crawled seductively over to him. Maybe it was the cut. Or maybe Wolf was a big tipper, but apparently she thought Dog would be throwing more her way than the guy in the suit she'd just abandoned.

Knowing it was proper etiquette to tip if you took a seat at the rail, Dog pulled out a five and tossed it at her. She gave him a little attention, but soon returned to the suit, who began upping the amount of bills he showered her with. Dog grinned, content to sip his drink and wait for Sonny. Blondes had never really been his type anyway, although he had to admit she had a nice rack. Her show was soon over, and she exited the stage to move through the crowd selling lap dances.

The music changed, and the flashing light show dimmed as another dancer took the stage. This one had a different style, and Dog could tell at a glance her show wouldn't be about any acrobatic pole work. She was a petite Asian beauty with long silky dark hair that hung to her waist. She was holding two large fans made of peacock feathers that hid her body. She danced and twirled, giving a teasing glimpse of different body parts, but never showing everything at once. It was erotic as hell, and Dog felt himself falling completely under her spell. As her dance continued, bills flew on to the stage from all directions, but she ignored them, totally caught up in her dance. She had a graceful way of moving that enticed and seduced. Unlike a lot of strippers, this dancer had skills that hinted at years of training. Ballet would be Red Dog's guess.

She made no eye contact with any of the men, which was another thing that separated her from the rest. Until toward the end of the dance as she did her floor work, laying on her back, writhing and moving her body in a sensual way that called out to every man there.

And then she rolled her head, and her eyes opened. They connected with Red Dog's, and he was blown away by the vivid green shade that stared back at him. Holding his gaze, she slowly twisted toward him, and then her shapely leg extended, her delicate bare foot landing on his chest. No tacky stripper shoes, another thing that set her apart. Dog had to admit he found her bare foot a thousand times sexier. His eyes fell to the pretty painted toes sliding up his leather cut as she arched her foot, then they climbed slowly up her leg, over the pearlescent skin of her slender body, to those vivid green almond shaped eyes. And she had him, hook, line and sinker.

As he watched, feeling like they were the only two people in the club, the pink tip of her tongue came out to glide over her lip.

Fucking hell.

She twisted and moved to her hands and knees, and crawled seductively toward him. Picking up one of her folded fans, she teased it over his chest, neck and the side of his face. Then, tossing it aside, she sat back, kneeling before him, her heels tucked under her ass and her back straight. She bowed her head, her palms flat on top of her thighs, and in that moment, Dog could think of nothing he wanted more than to have her kneel like that at his feet.

Jesus H. Christ what was this woman doing to him? He'd never had a reaction to a stripper like this before.

As he watched, her palms slid slowly up her body over her hips, her waist, to close over her small but perfectly shaped breasts. And then her head lifted, and her eyes connected with his as she squeezed and played with her tits.

Dog held two fingers out, a folded hundred-dollar bill between them. She moved toward him, her eyes getting big when they landed on the denomination. Her gaze snapped to his eyes as she reached for it. He held on to it a moment as he leaned forward to whisper, "Worth every penny, China Doll."

She moved on and soon finished her act.

Dog felt a hand on his shoulder and looked up to see Sonny. The man jerked his head, indicating Dog should follow him. He stood and moved off as the next dancer's pounding beat filled the room. They moved through a door and down a hallway, the music fading several decibels.

"Sorry to keep you waiting," Sonny said over his shoulder.

Dog glanced in an open doorway to the right and saw a bunch of dancer's changing. "No problem, Sonny."

"Things get crazy at the end of the night. Had to deal with some shit."

Sonny moved through another doorway into a small office. He bent and opened a safe and pulled out an envelope, handing it to Red Dog. It was stuffed thick with bills.

"We had a good week. Mack should be real

happy," Sonny remarked, referring to the club's President.

Dog tested the weight of the envelope before tucking it into his vest. "Good to know. Always like to keep the Prez happy."

"Things going well with the club?" Sonny lifted his chin toward Red Dog's Evil Dead cut.

"Always."

"Good to know." Sonny grinned, giving Red Dog's words back to him. "You parked out back?"

"Yeah, why?"

"Tell Tony the girls will be out in a minute."

"Will do. Take it easy." Dog moved down the hall to the door at the end that led to the back parking lot. Sure enough, Tony, who worked security for Sonny, was standing out there. "How's it going, man?"

Tony nodded to the puddles dancing with raindrops. "Storm's blowing in."

"Fucking El Niño."

Tony grinned. "Guess it sucks to ride in the rain."

"Yup." Dog folded his arms and leaned against the wall under the eave. "Maybe if I wait a few minutes, it'll ease up."

Tony eyed the sky. "Maybe."

"Sonny said the girls will be out in a minute."

"Yeah, it was kind of dead tonight. They'll be eager to go home."

About ten minutes later, two dancers came out the door and headed to their cars. One was the blonde; the other was the pretty little Asian girl he'd given the hundred bucks to, his little china doll.

"Goodnight, Tony," they both said as they dashed through the rain to their cars.

"Goodnight, ladies. Drive safe."

Dog ignored the blonde, his eyes only for the other dancer. The blonde got in her vehicle and pulled out. The other girl got in her car, but didn't start it.

"I hate when she does that," Tony muttered.

"What's that?" Dog frowned toward the white Mustang that just sat there.

Tony lifted his chin at the car. "Hangs around, texting or making calls. I've told her repeatedly that's not safe to do at night. She goes to her car, whether it's here or anywhere, she needs to get inside, lock the door, start it up and go, not sit around. But does she listen? Hell, no."

"You had problems here?"

"You never know when a patron is going to hang around, thinking he can hit on the dancers when they finish their shifts, or follow them home."

"You get many of those?"

"More than I'd like. The worst are the ones that get obsessed with one girl. They practically stalk them."

It was Dog's turn to lift his chin toward the Mustang. "She got any of those?"

"One guy lately. That's him over there in the blue sedan."

Dog's brows shot up. "You're shitting me, right? You let him just hang here?"

"It's a fine line I've got to walk. Can't be running them off. Those types can be some of these girls' best customers. The girls themselves would string me up if I came between them and their income."

"You're here to protect them. That is your fucking job."

Tony nodded. "I make sure he doesn't approach or

follow her out of the parking lot."

"Well, since he's not getting out of his vehicle, I'm guessing the latter."

"Yup. Guess I better go have a talk with him." Tony moved to step out from under the eave and into the rain, when the back door opened and a brunette stuck her head out.

"Tony, Sonny needs you. He thinks Tiffany is OD'ing.

"Jesus Christ. Again?"

The brunette shrugged her shoulders and ducked back inside. Tony grabbed the door to follow, but paused nodding toward the white Mustang. "Can you make sure she gets out of here okay?"

Red Dog nodded. "Yeah, sure, man. Go."

Tony ducked inside as a flash of lightning cracked across the sky, and the rain became a downpour. Dog watched as the Mustang's headlights came on, and a plume of exhaust shot out the tailpipe. His gaze swung to the blue sedan. It was backed into a spot, and with the rain pouring down on the windshield Dog couldn't make out the driver's face, just a dark shadow. His eyes cut back to the Mustang to see it backing out, then moving toward the street and turning right out of the parking lot. As the sedan pulled from its spot, Dog darted out, moving to step in front of the vehicle. Their eyes connected through the windshield, and this time Dog could see the man's features. He was a squirrely looking dude, but it was what Dog saw in his eyes that had his blood running cold. Evil, pure fucking evil, with no emotion in them.

Red Dog banged his palm on the hood and barked, "Get the fuck out of the car."

A twisted smile formed on the man's face a split second before he gunned the engine, plowing into Dog. The impact knocked him off his feet and up onto the hood, where he rolled and fell to the ground as the car sped away.

Dog groaned at the pain that shot through his left leg, which had taken the brunt of the impact. But that didn't stop him from rolling to his knees, drawing his gun and firing as the car turned right, tires squealing as it barreled off the lot.

Boom. Boom. Boom. The sound of his gun echoed off the building. A moment later, the door flew open and banged against the cement block wall as Tony charged out. He skidded to a stop, his eyes taking in Dog's kneeling position, the 9mm clenched in his hand aimed at the street.

"What the fuck happened?"

"He got away. He's going after her. Where the hell does she live?" Dog barked as he staggered to his feet, favoring his left leg, then holstered his gun as he moved toward his bike.

Tony pulled his phone out. "Let me call her. Tell her she's got a tail and to come back to the club."

Dog stood there a moment, his eyes on Tony, praying she'd pick up the man's call. Tony shook his head as he barked an order into what must have been her voicemail. "Don't get out of the car, Sweetie. You got a tail."

"Where?" Dog demanded, already firing his bike up.

"Royal Hill Apartments on Ocean Blvd. #814."

Red Dog roared off the lot, heading right.

By the time Dog found the address and followed the maze of turns through the complex to building eight, the guy already had her by the throat pressed up against her car door, but turned his head when he heard the Harley roar up.

Dog skidded to a stop on the wet pavement. He dropped the kickstand and dismounted, charging the man who pulled the girl in front of him and put a knife to her throat.

"Stay the fuck away or I'll slice her," he threatened.

Dog pulled his gun and aimed it at the man's head. "You do, it'll be the last fucking thing you ever do."

Dog watched as the man's face paled, then he shoved the girl at him and took off running. Dog caught her to him as he watched the man disappear into the darkness. The motherfucker had left his car behind; therefore he wouldn't be hard to hunt down. Looking at the trembling woman in his arms, he asked, "You okay, China Doll?"

She nodded, looking up at him.

"Let's get you inside."

Once he had her in out of the rain, he pulled out his phone and made a call to his club. That little knife-wielding fucker wouldn't survive the night. Dog peered through the curtains to the parking lot. He'd paused long enough to slash the tires on the sedan, making sure the man didn't return for it.

Dog let the curtain drop and turned back to see his little dancer was shaking. "You look like you could use a drink, honey. You got anything?"

She nodded towards the kitchen area where a low bar overlooked the living room and whispered, "There's a bottle of wine in the fridge."

The corner of his mouth pulled up. "Think we may need something a little stronger, sweetheart. Got any liquor?"

"A bottle of tequila in the cabinet over the sink."

Dog nodded and moved off to get it. He returned to her a minute later and held out a rocks glass with a two finger shot in the bottom. "Drink up."

She took it and downed it. "I suppose I should thank you, but I don't even know your name."

He took the glass from her and refilled it from the bottle he held. Handing it back to her, he replied, "My friends call me Red Dog."

Her pretty little brow frowned. "Red Dog?"

He nodded, a grin pulling at the corner of his mouth. "Yeah. And you're welcome."

She drank the second shot. "How did you find me?"

He took the glass from her, sat on one of the barstools, and poured himself a shot. Then he told her what had happened after she'd pulled out of the club.

"Oh, my God. Are you hurt?" She took a step toward him.

"I'll be limping for a couple days, but I'll survive."

"I'm so sorry." Her eyes fell to his cut, and she nodded toward it. "You're not the guy that usually comes around for Sonny."

"Nope. Just my lucky night." He tried to joke with her.

She frowned. "Where's the other guy? Wolf."

"He had business to take care of tonight." Dog's eyes narrowed. "How well do you know him?"

She shook her head. "I don't. Not like that."

Dog nodded. "You want me to call anyone for you?

Tony?"

She shook her head again. "No, I'll be fine."

"Bullshit."

"Excuse me?"

"You heard me."

"I can assure you I've had stalkers before. It comes with the job."

"And a knife at your throat? You have that before, too?"

At that she swallowed and looked away, lifting her chin. "I have a gun. I'll be fine."

"Yeah? And where was that gun when he had you pinned against your car?"

She looked back at him and admitted, "In my purse."

"Where it did you absolutely zero good."

They stared at each other a long moment, and then her eyes dropped, taking in his clothes. "You're soaking wet."

"So are you." He lifted his chin at her, his eyes sweeping over her. "You should go change out of those clothes before you catch your death."

She had on a sleeveless red satin dress, the kind with a high collar that looked oriental and suited her perfectly. As he watched, she hiked up the hem exposing a garter around her thigh. He watched her slender fingers — with their red-painted nails — slip a wad of cash free. She pulled out the hundred-dollar bill he'd given her and held it out to him. "I think you earned this back tonight."

His eyes had a hard time pulling away from that garter to meet her eyes. When he did, he saw a hint of vulnerability flash for a moment, before the tough girl act returned, and she lifted her chin. He relaxed back. "Keep it. Told you, worth every penny."

She dropped the hand she'd held out. "Okay, fine."

He watched her move to a carved wooden box sitting on a shelf in a bookcase. She opened it and shoved the wad of cash that she'd taken from her garter inside. Red Dog noticed the bills joined a tall stack already stored in the box.

"You don't seriously keep your money in that, do you?" Red Dog asked in amazement.

She glanced over at him as she closed it. "Until I get to the bank and put it in my savings account, yes."

Red Dog noted she'd said savings, not checking. "Saving up for something special?"

She nodded.

"And what would that be?"

"Do you really care?"

"Yeah, I really care," he replied, amazed by his own answer.

She clasped her hands behind her back and took a step toward him. "You won't laugh?"

Red Dog frowned. "Why would I laugh?"

She lifted her chin. "I'm saving up to open a dance studio."

"A dance studio?"

She nodded, and something in her expression conveyed to him that she wanted his approval.

"What exactly is a dance studio?"

"I would teach children how to dance. Beginning ballet, tap and jazz dance."

Red Dog nodded. "I thought you looked like you had real dance training."

At the reminder of the dance he'd seen her do she

looked away. But then she lifted her chin and met his gaze directly. "I've never seen you come around before."

"Not my usual gig." His eyes studied hers, his head tilting. "When did you start working for Sonny?"

"Two months ago."

"You must do well. That was quite an act."

Her chin came up again. "I do okay."

Dog nodded slowly. "Hottest thing I've ever seen."

He could see in her eyes, she didn't know how to take him. But she wasn't afraid of him, which most women would be. He lifted his chin.

"C'mere, China Doll."

"I have a name." She took a step toward him. He reached out and took her hand, pulling her to stand between his spread legs. Then his hands landed on her satin covered hips. When her eyes met his, he saw interest not fear, so he dipped his head and covered her mouth with his. She didn't pull away; in fact she melted against him, her hands sliding up to his neck. He kissed her softly, gently, brushing her lips with kiss after kiss. But she wanted more, and she pulled his head back down each time he pulled back from a kiss, until she was following him, going up on her tiptoes to maintain the contact.

Red Dog stood, his big hands moving to her ass as he lifted her up. Her dress hiked up as she wrapped her legs around his waist. He walked her down the hallway, past a bathroom to the only bedroom. He didn't bother with the light switch; there was enough light coming from the hall.

He broke the kiss long enough to glance around the room. A brass bed with a girly flowered comforter. It was full size, plenty big enough for her, but not near enough for him. That didn't matter; he'd make do. He laid her across it and came down on top of her. Then one hand slid under her back reaching for the zipper of her dress. He pulled it down slowly, watching her eyes closely for any reaction, any indication that she wanted him to stop or to slow down. He saw none.

Still, he didn't want her to feel pressured, so he rolled until she was on top, letting her have the opportunity to climb off if she'd changed her mind.

Apparently she hadn't, because as he watched, she sat up, straddling his hips and pulled the dress over her head. His big palms slid to her waist as he took her in. Demure pink lace bra and panties hit his eyes, more feminine than sexy, but perfect with her pearly skin and long dark hair that fell in a sheet over one shoulder. He reached up and let the silky strands slide through his fingers.

"You're beautiful," he murmured. And then he reached for her hand, bringing it to his mouth where he kissed each fingertip. "You're not scared of me, are you?"

She stared down at him, watching intently as his mouth moved to her palm, and then she whispered, "Should I be?"

"No. Never be afraid of me, China Doll. Never."

"Then I won't."

He reached up, hooked a hand at the nape of her neck and pulled her gently down. "C'mere, baby."

When their mouths met, he rolled again, taking her to her back and lifting up on one elbow. He stared down at her, and then his eyes moved to her comforter that was now damp from his wet clothes. He grinned.

"Oops."

She turned her head to look, and they both started laughing.

"Maybe you should take off your wet clothes," she suggested.

He grinned and lifted off her to stand at the foot of the bed and strip.

"Sexy," she teased. "But, slower, hot-stuff. Shake that ass. I've got some dollar bills in my purse. Maybe I should get them."

"Think that's funny, baby doll? You like to tease, do you?"

He finished quickly and came down on top of her, pinning her to the bed. He silenced her laughter with a kiss. And then his eyes fell on a vase on her nightstand. It was filled with peacock feathers, which reminded him of the dance she'd done. He leaned across her, stretching out an arm to grab one. Then he brought it to her skin, dragging it slowly across her breasts and belly.

She giggled and squirmed.

"Shh, hold still now, baby." She quieted, and he continued his journey down to her toes and back, his eyes watching the tiny goose bumps that formed wherever he touched. "You like this?"

She tossed her head on the pillow, trying to hold in her laughter. "It's torture."

He grinned. "You're the one with the feathers next to your bed, not me. Besides, you gave me all kinds of ideas with that fan act of yours."

"You didn't like it?"

"I loved it. Sexy as hell." He put his head in his hand, his elbow in the bed and continued tormenting her waist and breasts with the feather. "Know what I liked best?"

Her head turned to him, her eyes lifting from watching the feather to meet his. "What?"

Her voice was breathless. He liked that. "When you slid that pretty little foot of yours up my chest."

Her palm cupped his jaw, her thumb grazing his lower lip as one foot began to stroke up and down his calf. "Can we quit playing now?"

He grinned, nipped at the pad of her thumb and tossed the feather aside. Then he moved over her. "Whatever the lady wants."

Cole's voice shook him from his memories, pulling him back to the present.

"Where would she go, Dog? Think."

Suddenly he surged to his feet. "Let's go."

The men followed him as he stomped down the hall and out the front door.

"Where we goin'?" Cole asked as they all fired up their bikes.

"To get wontons!" Dog yelled before twisting his throttle and roaring off down the street.

"Say what?" Wolf asked Cole.

"Did he say wontons?" Green asked, frowning. "What the fuck does that mean?"

"Hell if I know. Just shut up and come on."

"He's starting to go off the rails," Wolf said, his eyes on the road in the direction that Red Dog had disappeared.

Cole nodded. "Yeah, well if we want to stop that from happening, then we'd better find Mary, and do it quick."

CHAPTER FOUR

As Red Dog roared across town, his bike rumbling beneath him, he thought back to how happy he and Mary been that first year.

They'd practically been inseparable.

Fourteen years ago...

Red Dog lay in bed with Mary. He stared at the ceiling, his mind on the fact that he had to leave town for about ten days for the club's annual run to Sturgis Bike Week in South Dakota. It was mandatory.

His hand stroked her back as he wondered how he was going to tell her.

"I've been thinking about getting a tattoo," she confessed in a whisper, drawing his attention away from the problem.

He frowned, cocking his head. "A tattoo? Why?"

"Because I want one."

"Mary, your skin is flawless. It's like porcelain. Why do you want to mark it?"

"Because there's something I want to get. I've been thinking about it for a while now. Don't be mad, okay?" She started to pout, and he felt himself giving in.

"Where did you want this tattoo?"

"On my back."

He trailed the back of his fingers over her skin, his mind more on his coming trip than the tattoo. "I've got to go out of town for about a week."

She lifted up to look at him. "You do?"

He nodded. "Sturgis. It's a mandatory run, our national meeting. I can't get out of it."

"Oh."

"I hate I have to leave you." He brushed the hair back from her forehead, studying her eyes. "You know that, right?"

She nodded. "I'll miss you."

"I'll miss you, too. First time I've ever dreaded the Sturgis run." He grinned.

She smiled back, teasing, "Maybe if you play your cards right, I'll still be here when you get back."

His brows shot up, and he chuckled. "Oh, you better still be here, China Doll."

She laughed and rested her head back down on his chest.

"Tell me about this tattoo you want to get."

"Uh-uh. I want it to be a surprise."

"Who's gonna do the work?"

"The work?"

"The ink, baby. Who's doing it?" He glanced down and watched her little brow furrow.

"I hadn't gotten that far."

"Well, when you do, I know a guy."

"You do?"

"Yeah, one of my club brothers." He lifted his arm,

showing her some of his tattoos. "He does all my ink. He used to have a shop. Just does it on the side, now."

"Will he give me a deal?" she teased up at him.

"Pretty as you are, he'll probably do it for free."

"Sold."

He grinned. "He's my brother, so he touches you, I'll kill him. You understand?"

She chuckled. "Got it, honey."

His eyes suddenly narrowed. "You know, they say tattoos can be addictive. You get one, you're gonna want another."

"Hmm." She glanced down at her chest.

"He's not tattooing your tits, babe."

"What's wrong with a tattoo there?"

"Nothing. They're fine. On another broad."

"Why not me?"

He ticked off his fingers. "One, I like your tits just the way they are. Two, nobody touches them but me. Three, my brothers *especially* don't touch 'em." His brows shot up. "We clear on that?"

"Yes, sir. Just the back."

He eyed her suspiciously. "I'd better like it."

She grinned back at him. "I think you're going to like it a lot."

"Property of Red Dog, that's what you should put."

"More special."

"Nothin' more special than that, China Doll."

"This will be."

And he remembered when he'd come back from that Sturgis trip...

Dog rode home, walked in the door and Mary jumped in his arms. He carried her, kissing her as he moved through to the bedroom, kicking the door shut with his boot. Then he set her down, his eyes taking her in. She was in a short kimono robe in vivid red silk. It tied at the waist. He wanted it off her, but he was dying to see the ink she'd gotten. Especially after having stopped off at the clubhouse and seeing the little grin on Crash's face when he looked at Red Dog.

Crash had been elected to stay behind and watch the clubhouse, partially because he'd busted up his leg that year and was hobbling in a cast.

"What did you do?" Dog had barked at him.

"What you asked me to do."

"And?"

"And what? It's some of my best work."

"I'm gonna like it?"

"How the fuck should I know?"

"Crash—" Dog started in a threatening tone.

"You *better* like it, that's all I'm sayin'."

"What's that supposed to mean?"

"It means, if you're a smart man, you'll tell her you love it, whether you do or not. She did it for you. Not sure what the fuck it means, but she said you'll understand."

And that had him worried. What if he *didn't* understand? What if the tattoo's meaning went right over his head?

So, here he stood, with her in nothing, *he hoped*, but that kimono, and all he could think about was that damn tattoo.

"Let me see." His voice came out gravelly, even to his own ears.

She turned, looking back at him over her shoulder as her hands undid the sash. She bit her lip as she let the robe slip slowly off her shoulders and down to pool on the floor.

His eyes took in the colorful art that covered her back. *Covered*. Her skin — from her shoulders all the way down to her ass — was inked. He'd expected something small, but not this. Somehow he shouldn't have been surprised. His Mary, he was learning, never did anything halfway.

He shouldn't have worried about what the tattoo's symbolism or meaning would be or if he'd get it. He got it. It's meaning was vividly clear in a vibrant rainbow of colors.

It was an image of a peacock, its tail down, sweeping low to curl over the top of one of her ass cheeks. Yes, it's meaning was clear to him. The dance she'd been doing the night he first met her, when she'd seduced him with those damn peacock feathers. The most erotic thing he'd ever seen. She still had a few of those feathers in a vase by her bed, ones he'd often used to stroke sensually over her soft skin on more than one occasion. So, yeah, the symbolism of her tattoo meant something between them.

As Dog's eyes trailed down over her perfect ass, a part of him wanted to strangle Crash for having tattooed her there. He could just imagine her laid out across Crash's table, her cute little ass half exposed and Crash with his head bent, putting a needle to her tender skin.

"Baby?" Mary called in a soft voice; shaking him from his felonious thoughts of all the ways he wanted to kill Crash.

"Hmm?" His eyes trailed back up to her face.

"You don't like it?"

He could see her eyes were practically shimmering, on the verge of tears.

"I thought you'd like it." Her voice trembled.

"I do, baby. I love it." His eyes softened. "C'mere."

She turned and moved to him.

He lifted her in his arms, and her legs wrapped around his waist. He moved toward the bed and paused before laying her across it. "Is it healed? Are you still sore?"

She shook her head. "It's fine."

He laid her back across the mattress, coming down on top of her and settling between her thighs. "I missed you, China Doll."

Her arms and legs wrapped around him, holding him close. "I missed you, too. So much."

CHAPTER FIVE

When the four bikes arrived at a house across town, Red Dog carried his Chinese takeout bag from Jimmy Wong's up the steps to the door. His brothers dismounted and stood watching him ring the bell.

A moment later an old Chinese woman came to the door.

"Where's your daughter?" Dog bit out.

She glanced past him to the bikes, and then her eyes returned to his as she snapped out in her chopped off accent, "Where my wontons? No wontons, no talk." She started to slam the door in his face, but Red Dog grabbed it with one hand and held the takeout bag up with the other.

A big grin formed on her face. "You always my favorite."

She made to reach for the bag, but Red Dog held it just out of her reach. "First you tell me where Mary went."

She made another grab for the bag, and he could hear his brothers trying to suppress their laughter behind him. He continued to hold it above her head, which wasn't hard to do since she was a tiny woman.

"Come on, Mama Wu. You want these, I need some info first."

She put her hands on her hips. "She came. She left."

"Where was she going?"

"She tell me nothing. She picked up the boy and left."

"Billy was here?"

She nodded.

Dog handed over the bag, pulled his phone out and tried his son, but it went straight to voicemail.

"I think she took his phone before she hauled him outta here," Mama Wu advised him. "What you do this time make my daughter so mad?"

"Hell if I know. You're daughter is crazy."

"Mary not crazy. You crazy. You find her," she ordered shaking a finger at him, and with that she slammed the door.

"Motherfucking hell." Red Dog sat down on the front step, not a clue where to start. He'd pinned all his hopes on the chance she'd just come home, or at the very least that her mother would know where she'd gone. But this? This he hadn't expected. That she'd just take off…

He thought back to all the rough spots they'd had over the years, all the heartache they'd dealt with. And they *had* dealt with it. And they'd come out the other side. Maybe not without a few scars, but they'd made it. Or at least he'd thought they had.

Dog remembered it like it was yesterday. They'd loved each other so much. In the early days when everything was good, Dog never imagined anything could come between them. That was before Mary had her first miscarriage, and then her second, and a third.

With each one, he felt her pull away, drifting away to a dark place where he couldn't reach her no matter how much he tried. And then the guilt settled deep inside him. Red Dog was a big man. Six four in height. While Mary was as petite as they came. And the thought gnawed at his gut that he was to blame, that she was just too small to carry the child of a big man like him. No matter how much the doctors reassured him that it had nothing to do with that, he still couldn't let that thought go. It nagged at his brain.

And he feared that perhaps she felt guilt, too. Guilt that she couldn't carry the babies, guilt that she couldn't give him all the children they'd both dreamed about and talked about in the early days, lying snuggled together in bed late at night.

Somehow, they'd moved past it and eventually had their son, Billy. And they were happy, so happy. And for years they hadn't tried again, believing that the child that God had given them would be enough.

Until one summer several years ago when that all changed. Mary had gotten pregnant again. Only this time she hadn't told him. He'd gone out of town for Sturgis that year, and she'd had another miscarriage. But this time he wasn't there for her. He knew nothing of the hell she was going through alone.

She had never told him of the pregnancy or the miscarriage.

And then when he returned, she began to push him away, and they grew more and more distant from each other. Red Dog had no idea why or what he had done. And so, as weeks turned into months, his frustration had grown. Mary seemed to grow colder and more indifferent to him with each passing day, until eventually he'd turned and sought out comfort with one of the women who hung around the club, a woman who had meant nothing to him. It had been wrong to do, and he knew it.

It wasn't until after Mary found out about it and confronted him, that she finally confessed that she'd had another miscarriage, and that it was the reason she'd pushed him away and put up a wall between them.

He'd been devastated, filled with remorse and regret and crushed by guilt. Not only for not being there for her and not going through it with her, but also for letting her push him away without a fight, for not forcing her to tell him what was wrong between them.

It had taken them a lot of work to rebuild what they'd lost, but they had. They'd come so far.

So how could she throw it all away?

And how could he ever live without her?

Suddenly, he felt the blood drain from his face. Oh, God. Was it possible she'd had another miscarriage? Jesus Christ, he had to find her.

He surged to his feet. "I've got to go look for her."

"Yeah, but where?" Cole asked him.

"I don't know, but I've got to find her."

Cole grabbed his shoulder. "All right. We'll find her, Dog. I promise. If we have to get everybody out lookin' —"

They were interrupted by Red Dog's ringtone. He yanked it out of his pocket, praying it was Mary. Glancing down at the screen, he saw it was Crash.

He put him on speaker. "Yeah?"

"What the hell did you do? It's Saturday morning, which means I should be in bed with my wife's legs wrapped around me. Instead, I'm up making my own damn coffee, while your wife is upstairs complaining to mine about you. So again, I ask, what the hell did you do?"

Dog felt relief surge through him. "I'll be right over. Don't let her leave." He jammed his phone in his pocket and headed for his bike.

"Let's roll, boys," Cole ordered.

"You don't have to come along. Think I can take it from here," Red Dog said as he strapped on his helmet.

Cole chuckled. "And miss seeing you grovel? No way in hell."

Red Dog rolled his eyes. "Asshole."

"That's what brothers are for, Dog. Always here to laugh and point when you're getting your nose rubbed in it."

"Fucking hell. Then, let's go."

The four bikes roared off down the street, headed toward Oakland.

CHAPTER SIX

Forty miles later, the bikes pulled up to a brick two-story building that had once been a manufacturing company. In old peeling paint on the side were the words, *Amalgamated Machine Works*, and below it in smaller script were the words, *Machining Since 1885*.

They parked at the curb near a garage door in the side of the building.

Knowing the place was locked up like a fortress, Red Dog pulled out his phone and called Crash. "You want to raise the garage door for us?"

"That depends. Did you bring donuts?"

"No, I didn't bring fucking donuts, asshole. Let me in."

"Nope. Not without donuts. The good kind."

"Are you fucking serious right now?"

"Serious as a heart attack, bro."

Dog pulled his phone away from his face and stared down at it. "He fucking hung up on me."

"What's the matter?"

"The motherfucker wants me to bring him donuts."

That got a snicker from Wolf and a snort from Cole.

"I could go for a donut," Green remarked, a glazed

over look on his face. "The chocolate frosted kind with sprinkles."

Their gazes all swung to him.

He refocused his eyes on them. "What? I like sprinkles. Sue me."

Dog whipped out a twenty and shoved it at him. "Run down the street and get a fucking dozen, then get your ass back here pronto."

"What? Me?"

"Just fucking do it."

Ten minutes later, only when Dog assured Crash that he had chocolate frosted payment in hand, did the steel door slowly roll up deeming them entry into what the boys lovingly referred to as *The Batcave*.

Dog eyed the black '68 Plymouth GTX parked in the ground-floor garage. Mary's car, the one he'd bought her for her birthday a couple years back. With its 375 horse power big block, 440 cubic inch V-8 engine under the hood, it was a much sought after muscle car and seriously impressive out on the open road. Of course, what Mary loved about it was its sleek lines, shiny 14" rally wheels, and its pretty black paint job.

His son, on the other hand, loved *all* those things and seriously had his heart set on assuming the keys when he turned sixteen in about fourteen months.

Gazing in the backseat, Dog noticed it was packed full.

Fucking hell.

The men loaded onto the metal freight elevator. Cole slammed the gate shut and threw the lever that had the shaky contraption ascending slowly, the brick wall sliding past them visible through the iron bars.

The old thing creaked and groaned as it slowly rose.

Red Dog glanced back to see Green had the donut box open and half of one already eaten, chocolate glaze all over his face. "Seriously?"

"What?" Green asked around a mouthful. "I was hungry."

Cole barely threw the lever into the stop position before Dog was flinging the gate open with a bang and charging out. The others followed him, stepping into Crash's loft.

Crash had remodeled the old building into an eclectic industrial loft. The walls were brick; the ceilings were a good thirty feet high with exposed iron beams and skylights staggered between them at intervals. The floor was a polished concrete.

There was a pool table to the left, a light hanging over it, beyond that was an open kitchen with a huge granite island. Funky industrial pendant lights hung over it. Across, off to the right was a large U-shaped sectional sofa, a coffee table and a couple of overstuffed chairs grouped around a thick brightly colored area rug that gave the place some color.

Dog moved past the pool table to the granite island where Crash stood sipping on a cup of coffee.

"Where is she?" Dog barked.

Crash eyed him calmly and then asked, "You bring donuts?"

Dog reached back, snatched the box out of Green's hands and tossed it on the island with a bang.

Crash eyed it and grinned, taking another sip of coffee.

"You gonna tell me where my goddamn wife is?" Dog growled.

"You calm your ass down, I will." Crash's eyes slid to the side and Dog's followed.

Billy, Dog's son, sat on the sectional, his back slumped against the backrest, and Crash's three year old daughter bouncing on his lap, her fists held in both his hands. He was laughing at her.

Dog's eyes took in his son, realizing just how grown up he was getting. His lanky frame was already starting to show signs of his father's long legs, tall height and broad shoulders. He'd inherited his mother's dark silky hair that was beginning to grow past his collar. He wore it tucked behind his ears, and Dog knew it was because he wanted to grow it out. He also had his mother's vivid green eyes.

He was fourteen now, that age when a boy started to become a man, an age when he needed his father more than ever. And Dog had no intention of letting him down. He would keep this family together no matter what the cost.

"You need to calm down before you talk to her. Take a breath. Your son is watching, bro."

Dog ran a hand down his face and blew out a breath.

"You okay?"

"Yeah."

Green picked up a glass pitcher from the island and sniffed it. "Mmm. Mimosas." Then he moved to the cabinet to take down a glass.

"Help yourself, why don't ya?" Crash offered sarcastically.

"Thanks, don't mind if I do," Green replied, already pouring one. He took a big chug from his glass and grinned. "Breakfast of champions."

Crash shook his head at Green and looked back at Dog. He held up a set of car keys. "Your boy was smart. Wouldn't let her drive. She wanted to go to Albuquerque. What the fuck's in Albuquerque, Dog?"

"Fuck if I know."

"Billy drove here instead. She was pissed, tried to get the keys from him. I took them and put a stop to that. She's up on the roof. Shannon is talking to her."

Dog took the keys. "Thanks."

He moved to stand next to his son. As he crossed the space, he vowed silently to himself that he would keep this family together no matter what the cost. It was a promise he sealed with a hand to his son's shoulder and a kiss to the top of his head. Yeah, he was a big bad biker, but he loved his son and wasn't afraid to show it.

Billy looked up. "She's pissed, Dad."

Dog nodded. "I know."

"You gonna fix it?"

"I'm gonna fix it."

"Promise?"

"You got my word, Son."

"I do not want to live with Grandma Wu. I mean, I love her and all, but…"

"I know, Son. That's not gonna happen."

"You sure? Cause it's lookin' that way."

"How'd you end up here?" Dog asked, wanting to hear his son's version.

"She left me over there last night so she could go out. She showed up early this morning and woke me up. Gram and Gramps weren't even up yet. Dragged me outside, had the car already loaded with shit and everything."

Dog frowned. "Where the hell was she going?"

Billy shook his head. "I could tell she'd been drinking, so I took the keys from her. She threatened to leave if I didn't give them back. Said she'd just start walking. I didn't know what to do, so I got behind the wheel. Told her I'd drive her wherever she wanted to go if she'd just get in the passenger seat and stop trying to grab the keys. She finally did, and we got up on the interstate."

"You don't even have your permit yet," Dog reminded him of something he knew the boy didn't need reminding of.

"I know how to drive, Dad."

"And where the hell did she want to go?"

He shrugged. "I'm not sure if she even knew. She told me to drive to Albuquerque."

"Albuquerque? What the hell's in Albuquerque?"

Billy shrugged again. "Hell..." he glanced at the Crash's daughter. "I mean, heck if I know. I think it was the first thing that popped in her head. I drove her here instead. Boy, was she pissed about that." He shook his head. "I figured Crash could help me settle her down until you showed back up. I didn't know what else to do, Dad."

"You did good, Son. You did the smart thing." He patted his shoulder. "Did she seem sad to you?"

Billy frowned. "No. Just pissed. Why?"

Dog shook his head. "Never mind, just trying to figure out what this is about."

"You gonna fix this? 'Cause now she's pissed at *both* of us."

"Don't worry, Son. I got this." They stared at each other. "You okay here for a minute?"

Billy, already wise beyond his years, lifted his chin toward the door to the rooftop, a slight grin pulling at his mouth. "Gonna take more than a minute, Dad, and we both know it."

Dog swiveled his head, following the direction of his son's gaze, and then he grinned back. "True."

Billy's eyes returned to the child bouncing on his belly.

"She likes you, huh?" Dog asked, squatting down and nodding toward Crash's child.

Billy lifted her up in the air over his head, and she squealed. "She's my best girl, aren't you, punkin'?"

When he dropped her back down, she pleaded in her baby voice, "Do it again. Do it again."

He tossed her up again to a fit of giggles.

Dog rubbed the top of his son's head and rose to his feet, his knees cracking. "Be back in a second."

"Yeah, sure. A second." Neither of them believed *that* lie. They exchanged a smile, and Dog moved off toward the stairs that led to the roof.

CHAPTER SEVEN

As Red Dog walked out onto the rooftop that overlooked the city and the Bay Bridge in the distance, Mary twisted to look from her seat on one of a pair of Adirondack chairs.

"What are you doing here? How did you find me?"

Dog strolled over to her. "How do you think?"

"My mother?"

He grinned down at her. "Told you before, she likes me better than you."

"How could she know where I was? *I* didn't even know I was coming here." Her eyes narrowed. "Did our son call you?"

"Nope. Guess again."

"Crash. He ratted me out?"

"You think he wouldn't?"

She rolled her eyes and glared over at Shannon, who sat in the chair next to her, as if it were her fault.

"Babe, don't be giving her the evil eye. None of this is her fault."

"That's right. It's yours. Now, get out. I've got nothing to say to you."

Red Dog looked over at Shannon. "Can you give

me a minute with my ol' lady?"

She stood to leave. "Of course."

Mary grabbed her arm. "Don't you dare leave."

Shannon looked between them, obviously wanting to protect her friend, the sisterhood and all that, but at the same time, hopefully having learned her lesson in the past about getting in Dog's business. "I..."

She was saved from having to betray her friend when Crash appeared in the doorway. "Shannon." He lifted his chin at her, an unspoken command to come to him.

She obeyed, thankful for the excuse to escape.

"Coward!" Mary yelled after her.

"Only coward I see is you." Red Dog stared down at her. "I'm six hours down the road when you pull this stunt. You wait until I'm so far away I can't do shit? Was that your plan? Well, how'd that work out for you?"

She sipped her drink, ignoring him. He took the glass from her hand and sniffed its contents. "Little early to tie one on, isn't it?"

"You're one to talk."

He set the glass down and squatted before her, bringing his face level with hers. "Guess we got some shit to work out, huh?"

She folded her arms and looked away. Dog studied her stiff posture. This was so totally not her usual M.O. that it threw him. Mary was always up for a knockdown, drag-out fight. She never gave him the silent treatment. Never. Goddamn, he must have really fucked up this time. He'd never seen her this hurt before.

"Mary, talk to me."

Still nothing.

Quietly he broached the subject, not really sure how to start. "You didn't... it wasn't another miscarriage was it?"

She looked off to the horizon.

"Baby?"

"No," she whispered. "Not that."

He blew out a relieved breath and studied her body language. She was telling him the truth. She was too pissed to be in that devastated dark place every previous miscarriage had taken her. No, this was something different. And judging by her mood, whatever had pissed her off was his fault.

"China Doll, you gotta tell me what the fuck I did."

Her chin went up, and her jaw clenched, but still she said nothing.

"I love you. You know that, don't you?"

No reaction. Nothing.

"I'll be damned if I'll let you break up this family. Especially when I don't even know the reason. And if you think I'll let you walk out on me, you've lost your mind."

"I'm not the one breaking up our family, you big oaf. You are."

He gritted his teeth. "I can't fix it, if I don't know what I did."

Her eyes flashed to his. "You know what you did. Don't play the innocent with me."

His frustration got the best of him. "Fucking hell. Don't start that 'you know what you did' bullshit. You women always think we men know when we've fucked up. We fuck up all the time, so no I don't know what the hell I did. Just fucking tell me, woman!"

She whipped out her phone. He watched with suspicious eyes as she pulled something up and held it out to him.

Christ, he was afraid to look. At a glance, it appeared to be a photo. Fuck, whatever he'd done, she had photographic evidence. He took the phone from her, turned it around and studied the image.

He frowned, trying to place the photo. It was a shot of him, sure enough, bent down next to a car, changing a tire. Who the hell would take a picture of him changing a tire? And why would that piss her off? And then it hit him. *Motherfucking Rosalie.*

She was the club sweet-butt that Dog had cheated with. It had only lasted a couple of days before he'd ended it, and since then she'd been banned from the club.

"Babe, it's not what you think."

"Swipe to the next shot."

He moved his thumb across pulling up the next shot, a selfie with Rosalie in the foreground making a kissy face to the camera, and him in the background changing her tire. The caption read, *my man takes good care of me.*

That little bitch, she'd texted this crap to his ol' lady.

His eyes flashed up to Mary's. "This is bullshit, Mary."

Her brows shot up. "That's not you?"

He blew out a breath, his eyes closing for a moment. "Yeah, it's me, but I'm not her man. I'm not taking care of her. She's fucking with you, baby. That's all this is."

"Oh, I think somebody's fucking with somebody,

all right."

"So she feeds you a bunch of bullshit, and I don't even get the benefit of the doubt, no chance to explain? You don't come to me with this shit, you just up and leave me?"

"Yup."

"Babe—"

"I'm done."

Those were two words she'd never spoken to him. Not in fourteen years.

"Don't say that, Mary." He shook his head. "It's not what you think. It's not what she's makin' this out to be. I saw her broken down on the highway. She had her kid in the car. I put her spare on for her. End of story."

"Right."

"Baby, I swear to you, I'm done with her. She's been banned. I made sure of it. She's not allowed on club property anymore. You won't ever see her again. Ask any of the boys, they'll tell you. And I'll make sure she never does something like this again." He tossed her phone on the small side table. "I've been done with her for a long fucking time. And we already worked through that." He touched his jaw. "I've got the dental work to prove it."

She'd knocked his teeth out that time, and now he had five grand worth of dental implants in his mouth. She'd nearly broken his jaw, and he'd been lucky he hadn't had to eat through a straw for a month.

"Last time you thought I was fucking around on you, you met me at the door with a baseball bat. This time you just pack your shit and leave? That's not the woman I know. The woman I know is a fighter. She doesn't just roll over."

"Maybe I've had enough."

"Baby, I did *not* do what you think I did. I learned my lesson. I'm done with that shit, all of it. Been done with it for a long fucking time. I swear to you. I only want you."

She said nothing.

"After all we've been through, you're gonna sit there and tell me it's the end?"

She seemed totally unmoved by his argument, and that scared the shit out of him. For the first time in his life he began to fear he might really lose her, for real this time.

He swallowed and ran a palm over his face, a cold sick feeling forming in the pit of his stomach. Without her, he was nothing. She gave his life meaning. Yeah, he had the club, and he loved his brothers. But Mary was his center; she's what grounded him like nothing else in his life, not the club, not his brothers, not even Billy. Of course he loved his son, always would, but it was Mary who was the center of his world. Without her, he'd be a fucking mess. It'd all go to shit, all of it.

And he couldn't let that happen. So he'd better fucking tell her what she meant to him, and he'd better do it quick. He was a man, a biker, and therefore not good at this shit, but he knew he'd better man-up, swallow his pride and find the words. If it took baring his soul out here on this rooftop, then that's what he'd do.

He rose to his feet, grasped her hands and pulled her up. Then he took her face in his hands, and brought his down to within an inch of hers.

"I love you, Mary. You are my world, my life. You're everything to me. I swore to you I was done with that shit, and I am. The problems we had, we worked through them all. I haven't been with anyone else, and I promise you, *promise you* I never will. Do you understand me?"

She stared up at him, her eyes glazing. He knew she wanted to believe the words, but the hurt she felt ran deep.

"I swear to you, Mary, I did nothing with her. It's you I love. What you and I have, right here," he shook her. "It's special. Ain't found it with anyone else. Knew the day I laid eyes on you, you were the one for me. And I know I've screwed up in the past. I haven't always been there when you needed me most. And I know I don't fucking deserve you. But I'm asking you please, don't walk out on me."

"Dog—"

"Not lettin' you go. Not now. Not ever. You walk out that door; I'll find you and bring you home. No matter how far you run."

She stared up at him, saying nothing. Jesus Christ, was she really done with him?

"Do you still love me?" he asked, studying her eyes, searching, hoping he'd still see that love buried there somewhere.

When she didn't reply, he shook her. "Do you? You don't, I might as well take a walk off the edge of this roof right fucking now and get it over with, because I'm dead inside without you."

"Dog—"

"I'm not playin', Mary. You walk out on me, it'll break me. That what you want?"

She shook her head, tears rolling down her cheek. "I just want us to love each other."

"We do, baby. We do." He paused, his thumb brushing the tear away. "I know I've fucked up in the past. I know I put you through hell, but I'm done with all that. All the bad stuff that's happened to us, that's all in the past. I love you, Mary. You. I'd stop breathing if I didn't have you anymore. And I don't care if we never have another baby. I just can't lose *you*."

His mouth came down on hers. He tried to show her how he felt the only way he knew he was good at. The kiss was filled with all the feelings he didn't know how to communicate with words. It was soft and tender, and achingly gentle.

Finally, he broke off.

"I'm sorry I put you through all this." His eyes searched hers. "Forgive me?"

She stared back at him for the longest moment in his goddamn life before finally nodding and giving him the reprieve he'd been waiting for like some inmate on death row. And swear to God he felt his body deflate in relief. He pressed a kiss to her forehead, holding it for a moment as he thanked God for her. Then he took her into his arms and just held her close. Finally he pulled back to look into her eyes.

"Come on. Let's go home. We've got some makeup sex to get to."

Before she could say a word or disagree, he tossed her over his shoulder and headed for the door.

"Dog!" she shrieked. "Put me down."

He smacked her ass. "Nope. I'm takin' my woman home."

He carried her down into the loft.

The guys broke out in applause when they saw Dog hauling his ol' lady through the loft.

"Hey, Mary, did the boy sufficiently grovel enough?" Cole teased.

"He must have, she's goin' with him," Crash replied for her.

"Don't look like she's got a choice," Wolf observed.

Dog paused to look at his son. "You good to hang here for a few?"

Crash's daughter hugged his neck. "Yay!"

Billy tickled her. "I guess so."

"He's fine here, Dog," Crash advised him.

"We'll bring Billy home," Cole offered.

Wolf teased, "Yeah, we'll give you five minutes before we head that way. That should be enough time, right?"

Dog continued on his way, one hand holding Mary on his shoulder, and with the other flipping them all off.

"Make him earn it, Mary!" Green shouted.

"You boys need to shut up. All of you," Red Dog snapped as he carried his wife into the elevator and slammed the gate shut. It wasn't until they were descending that he set her on her feet.

He could hear the guys laughing, one of them shouting after them, "Make-up sex is the best!"

As the shaky old contraption descended, Red Dog backed Mary against the cage, his hands grasping the bars on either side of her head, corralling her in. Then his mouth came down on hers.

When the elevator reached the ground floor and stopped, he hefted her up and pressed her back against the bars as her legs wrapped around him. She moaned in delight as his mouth trailed down her throat. She began to slip, and he hefted her again, pinning her against the bars and shaking the entire elevator.

One of the guys yelled down, "We can hear you!"

They broke apart long enough to smile at each other. Dog twisted his head to look up the dark shaft to where one of them was shaking the gate and making lewd noises. He grinned back at Mary.

"Let's go home and do this right."

"I thought you were doing it pretty right," she teased him, her finger tracing his ear.

"Woman, don't tempt me. Or I *will* finish this right here." She tilted her head as if considering it, and he chuckled.

"A bed *would* be nice," she finally admitted.

"Damn straight." He tossed her up higher in his arms, so that he was looking up into her face. "I ever tell you how much I love you, China Doll?"

She gave him a soft smile. "I could stand to hear it a few more times tonight."

"Done."

He tossed her again and she clutched at him, shrieking like she thought he might drop her. "Red Dog!"

"Hold on to me, baby, and never let me go."

She smiled down at him and wrapped her arms around his neck.

He carried her off the elevator and took his ol' lady home.

EPILOGUE

Red Dog —

I poured shampoo in my palm and sank my hands into Mary's wet hair. The spray of warm water from the shower beat down upon her sexy back as I massaged her scalp, lathering the fragrant soap all through her long tresses. My eyes moved over the dark strands. I loved her silky hair, loved the way it felt between my fingers and the way if felt when it trailed across my skin every time we made love. Like it had just a few minutes ago when we'd done that very thing.

They say makeup sex is the best and they *are not wrong*.

I grinned at the thought, and she smiled back, looking up at me with her breasts pressed to my chest.

"What are you smiling at?" she asked.

"Just thinking about how awesome that sex was."

Her grin got bigger, and my eyes moved over her face, taking it all in.

"Are you happy?" I asked.

She nodded.

"I love you, China Doll." She meant everything to

me. There wasn't anything I wouldn't do for her.

She stared back at me with love in her eyes. "I love you, too, my big red-headed warrior."

"Even when I fuck up?"

She nodded. "Even then."

I lightly touched my lips to hers and then cupped water in my palm and sluiced it over her hair, rinsing the shampoo out, slowly, gently. I loved tending to her like this, loved that she let me do it.

"Did you see the way Billy was with little Harley Jean?" she asked almost absently, her eyes sliding closed as she enjoyed my ministrations.

"Yeah, she's a cutie, isn't she? And she sure loves him."

"I think she'll be coming of age right about the time Billy is old enough to be ready to settle down."

At that, I pulled back and looked down at my wife. "Momma, you lookin' to play matchmaker with those two?"

I watched her glistening shoulders shrug, droplets of water running down her breasts. "Why not?"

"It's a little early to be planning the boy's future."

"You *know* his future. The club."

I wasn't as positive as my wife. "The boy's fourteen. We've got a while, don't you think?" Then I paused, frowning, suddenly on to her game. "Wait a minute. It's grandbabies you're after, isn't it?"

She shrugged again, a small smile pulling at her lips. "Maybe."

I lifted my brows at her.

"Well, if I can't have another baby, I'll get one that way."

"I've got a better idea — let's keep working on

getting *you* pregnant again before you try to turn me into a grandpa — something I am *not* ready to be, by the way."

"Dog, we've tried."

I picked her up, shut the water off, and carried her to our big bed. Coming down on top of her, both our bodies wet, I grinned down at her. "I say we keep trying. I'm all for this trying stuff. You in?"

She rolled her eyes, grinned back and wrapped her arms around my neck, pulling me down to her for a deep kiss.

That was all the answer I needed. My baby was back, her arms around me, and I was never letting go again.

The End

If you enjoyed reading
Red Dog: An Evil Dead MC Novella,
please post a review on Amazon.

Visit my webpage for more
Evil Dead MC Stories
nicolejames.net

Made in the USA
Middletown, DE
18 October 2022